I0544916

PRINCIPLES
(Inspired by a true story)

SHAMICHAEL ELLIS

Principles

Copyright © 2021 by Shamichael Ellis

All rights reserved. This book or any portion thereof may not be reproduced or used in any manner whatsoever without the express written permission of the publisher except for the use of brief quotations in a book review.

Printed in the United States of America.

ISBN: 978-1-7372795-0-1

First Printing, 2021 Shreveport, LA 71119

www.mikeellisbooks.com

Principles

Featuring:

Michael Davis (Mike) or (Flukey Luke)
Jean-Jacques (RichBlood)
Katrina Lee
Roc
Alejandro
And a host of others

What are Principles?

By definition, principles are fundamental truths, beliefs controlling one's personal behavior or actions. They are all about your morality or the distinction between right and wrong.

Principles can also be rules.

I know that you've heard the saying that rules are made to be broken. While that may be true for some people, for others some rules are never meant to be broken. Usually, the people breaking the rules can afford the consequences. However, in the streets, when you break the rules, money doesn't always work. You see, it's not always about the money.

Sometimes it's just the principle...

Prologue

My name is Michael Rashad Davis, but everyone in my family calls me Flukey Luke. My parents gave me the nickname Flukey Luke after a cartoon character. He was a cowboy that usually got caught up in unfortunate circumstances, but no matter what, he always came out on top. My mom and pops must have predicted my future because my life eventually revolved around good luck and a few once-in-a-lifetime opportunities. I was born in Shreveport, Louisiana on May 20, 1977 at Confederate Memorial Hospital. I was raised in three of the worst neighborhoods my city had to offer a young black man. My father went to prison for a murder charge when I was young. He was always a hustler by nature, and he hustled his ass off.

Before my pops went to prison, he made sure my mom and I were financially straight for a while. We were okay for a bit. With the money he left, my mother used some of it to buy us a house in an area of the city called Queensborough. She used the rest to make sure there was always money kept on my pop's books. She also paid attorney fees to try to fight his case. My mother eventually got a job at a government ammunition plant in Minden, LA which was about a forty-five-minute drive from Shreveport. She worked

5

Principles

long hours to make ends meet, so that didn't leave a lot of time for me.

I'm the oldest grandchild on both sides of my family. Even though I was never a bad kid, I usually got away with the little things I did do. I was practically raised by my grandmothers, aunts, and uncles. One of my grandmothers lived in an area that we call Motown. That's the neighborhood where I met most of my childhood friends. I had six close friends that I grew up with, and the streets took away five of them. Two of my friends were gunned down and murdered. The other three got life sentences on charges that ranged from simple robbery to multiple homicides. Only two of us eventually made it out.

My other grandmother lived in Cedar Grove. This is where I spent most of my time as a youth. That neighborhood taught me about street life, survival skills, and how to hustle. My mother tried to shield and protect me from that life the best she could, but it was only so much she could do. At one point, my city was the murder capital of the United States for many years consecutively. According to recent FBI stats, Shreveport is still ranked number eight for being one of the most dangerous cities in the United States. By the time I was twelve years old, I'd already witnessed things like junkies overdosing, robberies, kidnaps, attempted murders, and

Principles

murders. You name it, and I've probably seen it.

Throughout my childhood and adolescence, my city seemed lawless. When my father was out on the streets, he and guys like him were part of the problem. My pops was a machine gun, two pistols toting, drug trafficking, murdering muthafucka. He was well respected in the city, but that came with a price. He mostly kept his street life away from my mother and me, but I can remember the day, the moment, and the only time I'd seen him kill someone... He had special ordered a Cadillac Fleetwood and decided to take me riding in it one day. I was so excited to be rolling with him.

While we were riding I can remember hanging my head out the sunroof and letting the wind blow through my hair as my father drove down Jewella Avenue. My dad and I never had much one-on-one time, so I was having the time of my life. However, it was short-lived. While I was enjoying the wind in my face and hair, my pops had gotten a phone call to meet up with someone. We ended up somewhere across town near a lot of beaten-up, abandoned houses. My dad said that he would just be a minute. He told me that he was leaving the car running and for me to make sure that I locked all the doors when he got out. Then, he approached some guy and started talking.

Principles

I recognized the guy my dad was talking to because I'd seen him before. He was one of my dad's associates named Bruce. Bruce was telling him about something that happened. I didn't hear the conversation, but I could tell that my pops was pissed. My dad started walking back towards the car, so I unlocked the doors. He got in, and we sped off like lightning. Within what seemed like ten or fifteen minutes, we arrived at what looked like a liquor store parking lot. My dad told me to put my head in my lap and close my eyes. I did exactly what he asked. The car door slammed shut. Then, I heard my father arguing with two men. I was curious to see what was going on, so I decided to take a peek.

By the time I raised my head, I heard the first gunshot. Then, I saw a blaze of fire from the barrel of the gun my father was holding in his hand. The first shot hit one of the guys somewhere in the upper body, spinning him around. I could see the man running across the parking lot. The second, third, and fourth shots ripped holes in the man's clothes and back. The other guy tried hiding behind a trash dumpster. When my father found the man and approached him, the guy put his hands to his face and began pleading and begging as if he was trying to bargain with the almighty God himself not to take his life. My pops shot the guy, and I could see his lifeless body drop to the ground in slow motion like a glass falling from a kitchen table. When my father returned to the car, he sat there for a second and made one statement to me.

He said, "Son, as long as you live, I want you to remember that a man is always judged on his principles. It's not always about the money. It's always about the principle. There are rules to this shit, and if you don't follow the rules, like it or not there will be consequences."

A week or so later, the police task force kicked in our front door and arrested my father. He went to prison where he would spend the rest of his life.

***

My city wasn't always full of murder, corruption, and chaos. We did have some good days. Fast forward to the summer of 1991... I was fourteen years old. It was a different time from where we are nowadays. Even though we had our share of drama as kids, we also had fun. My mom's side of the family is huge. Everyone in the city knew or had heard of the Dallas Family. I can remember walking to the neighborhood park with my aunts and uncles every weekend. The park was a big deal back then. We had break-dancing competitions, old school cars bumping loud music, low rider trucks with dancing truck beds, and best of all, the cookouts at the park. Those were the days.

Principles

It was probably in late '91 or early '92 when the dope flood gates had completely opened in Shreveport. One of the neighborhood corner boys named Kankey quickly became one of the biggest kingpins in the city. Kankey has always nickel and dimed here and there, but it seemed like he went from small-time to big-time in a matter of weeks. He had cocaine, heroin, weed, and anything else you wanted. From my understanding, Kankey was probably the first person in the city to take cocaine and rock it up. He even showed my Uncle Duck and Uncle Jimmy how to cook cocaine into crack, and they became really good at it.

My uncles started working for Kankey and business was booming. The three of them took care of the whole block of Abilene Street. They paid bills and put food on tables; no one needed anything. I can't even lie, the money was looking damn good. It looked so good, in fact, that I asked Kankey and both my uncles to put me down with some work on more than a few occasions. Each time they told me no, and every no also came with a motivational speech. They would always begin by telling me that the best view of the game was from my seat, so stay courtside.

As a kid, I never really knew what the fuck they meant by that. Every speech they gave me ended with "Stay in school. Go to college, and become a doctor, lawyer, or just do something productive with your life." But shit, little did I know, they had just as many rich ass doctors and lawyers coming through to buy dope as they had junkies. Nevertheless, I was always one of the brightest students at every school I had ever attended. There's absolutely nothing wrong with being the smart kid in school, but who wants to be smart and broke? See, the way I looked at it was that being smart and broke today only meant that I'd probably end up smart and broke tomorrow. And, that's not how I wanted to end up, so I had to improvise.

I've always known that I was a born hustler and thinker - more of a Renaissance man. Hell, I think I came out of my mother's womb with a hundred dollars and a dream. Everyone around me was shining and having nice things, and I wanted the same thing. From time to time, my Uncle Jimmy and Uncle Duck would send me inside my grandmother's house to get drugs or money for them. So, I knew exactly where they kept their stash. After a while, I started taking a little at a time to sell. I was stealing small amounts here and there. Uncle Jimmy and Uncle Duck had so many drugs that I didn't think either one would notice anything missing. I figured the worst-case scenario would be that if they did realize anything was missing, they would just blame each other and keep it moving.

Principles

With my new hustle, I was shining. I had money, and I stayed in fresh new clothes. I was feeling good and looking good. Nigga couldn't tell me shit until one day when my Uncle Jimmy caught me in the stash spot trying to steal more drugs to sell. I was caught red-handed. He told me that he and Uncle Duck had already known that it was me stealing from them the whole time. I didn't deny it. He told me that I gave myself away by flossing so much wearing the gold chains, watches, and rings with no job.

"Look Unc, I was born to do this shit," I said in my defense as I pulled out a wad of cash. "If I made this just off the little bit I've been getting from you and Uncle Duck, just imagine what I could do with some real product."

Uncle Jimmy said, "This shit is not for the faint of heart, nephew. You have to be ready to take a nigga head off his shoulder if need be. This is not the life that I wanted for you, kid, but it seems to me like you've already made up your mind. So, I'm not going to give a speech or preach to you about it. If this is really what you want to do, I can't stop you. It's your life, your choice, but let me explain one thing to you first..."

My uncle sat me down and asked, "Do you remember when we use to tell you that you had the best view of the game from your seat?"

"Yeah, I remember."

"Nephew, everyone's not going to be honest and keep it one hundred with you about the drug game. The game is two-sided like a deck of cards. On the winning side, there's the money, the women, the glitz, and the glamor. On the losing side, there's jealousy, envy, murder, and chaos."

I listened intently as he continued.

"Everyone seems to always glorify the winning side because no one really wants to acknowledge or talk about the losing side - the ugly side of the game. Whenever people begin to think you're winning, you'll become more of a target. You'll start seeing more haters and your fake friends and rivals will begin to envy you."

I took it all in as he continued to give me the truth about the game I wanted to be a part of so badly.

"Hell! Even though they may have hatred for each other, they'll come together just to make sure you don't succeed. Basically, kid, what I'm trying to tell you is that you have to be smarter than the opposition. You have to move as quietly as possible. Stop being flashy and shit. It draws too much attention."

"I feel you, Unc," I said.

"Nephew, I want you to be careful because one thing for certain is that every game has a beginning and an ending. Flukey, you're like a son to me. If you have any problems with anyone, let me know and I'll get shit handled for you." Unc grabbed a bag, reached in it, and gave me a brick of cocaine then said, "Now, go get paid, Nephew."

I started with that one kilo and all the right connections. My Uncle Jimmy put me down with Kankey. Once I gained Kankey's trust, I quickly graduated. I started moving brick by brick. Then, I began to move ten or fifteen kilos at a time. Eventually, I worked my way up to forty or fifty keys at a time. I was successful because I understood that good business goes a long way. I'd made rules for myself. I didn't step on anyone's toes. I never looked for drama or bullshit. If you didn't fuck with me, I didn't fuck with you. Last, but not least, it was all about respect. If you owe a man, you pay a man. If you don't have it, you go get it. No excuses.

Within two years, my operation had become too big for my small city, and I needed to expand to a much larger area. Dallas, Texas was my sweet spot. It made sense to me because I already had made connections in Dallas, San Antonio, and the surrounding areas. I had associates in the streets, on the police force, DEA, and politicians. Texas supported me, and I supported Texas.

***

Principles

I'm a strong believer when it comes to prayer and God. I've been in situations where I needed prayer. I've also been in situations where I had to pray for others. I believe we all want to be good people, but sometimes we just make bad decisions. From experience, I have also learned that there are some things you have to go through to make you who you are. I'm about to give you a more direct and personal glimpse into my life. I'm going to take you on a journey and show you the lessons and principles that I've learned along the way. One of my uncles once told me that if the drug business was the life I chose, just remember to bring a shovel because in the drug business shit can get waist-deep.

This is my life, my story, my words...

Lesson 1:
Teamwork Makes the Dream Work

There I was on a Thursday night sitting in a lounge, nightclub, or whatever the fuck you want to call it. I went there just to relax and have a couple of drinks with my family. I call my team my family because I don't have friends. I feel like you're either an associate or family, bottom line. My team works hard for me, so in return, I don't mind letting them play hard at my expense. I'm not really into the club scene. That's just never been my thing. I'll hang around for a couple of hours or so and then I'm gone in the wind. But, I know how to make sacrifices when necessary. My crew loves the nightlife, so I do it to see them have a great time.

Sometimes you have to give a little to get a lot in return. My crew isn't large simply because I prefer having a small circle around me. With a small circle, it's easier to tell who really will have your back if shit ever got ugly. Call me crazy, but in situations like that, I'd much rather have ten lions than a hundred sheep. I'll be the first to admit that I do have trust issues so I only have a few people that I can somewhat say I trust with my life.

First, there's Rocco. I call him Roc for short. Roc used to work for my pops, so I've known him since I was a kid. He's never been the type of guy to bullshit when it's about business. If he had to come to see you about business, he didn't come to play. He came to t-shirt yo ass. Roc has always been like a mentor to me, and now he's my distro for Atlanta and Los Angeles. Then, there's Alejandro. I call him Ale. He's only about five feet tall but make no mistakes about it; he can be as smooth as a butter knife or as savage as a machete. I met Ale eight years ago here in Texas at a fucking car show of all places. After getting to know him, I learned that cars weren't the only things we had in common. He's an absolute genius when it comes to wrapping and shipping products undetected. He's my distro for Texas and New York.

Last but not least, there's Nick. My boy works for the DEA, and he's my eyes and ears in that office. With him on my team, I have unlimited access to most of my competition. Whenever necessary, I know about every raid, shakedown, and snitch. With these three dudes on my team, my operation runs smoothly without a hitch. I trust them, and they trust me. That's why I don't mind-blowing a couple of stacks on them every once in a while which brings me here tonight.

While I was relaxing, enjoying the music and the atmosphere, the bartender handed me a drink that I didn't order.

I asked him, "What's up with the drink? I didn't ask for another one just yet."

Principles

"Look at the table behind you. The two ladies over there paid for this one, and they also covered your tab for the rest of the night."

I turned around to tell the ladies thanks, but they were signaling for me to come over to their table.

I asked the bartender, "Are they regulars in here?"

"I've never seen either one of them before."

I thanked him for the info and then walked over and tapped Roc on the shoulder. I pointed towards the table where the ladies were sitting and told him that I'd be over there if he needed anything.

He replied, "Okay, Flukey."

"Roc, why do I have to keep telling you the same thing over and over? Call me by my name. No one calls me Flukey anymore."

He laughed and took another sip from his glass as I approached the table where the ladies were sitting.

"How are you beautiful ladies doing tonight?"

Both women replied, "Thanks, we're fine."

"How are you tonight?" one of them asked.

"I'm good, but things can always get better."

While I was in the middle of a conversation with the two ladies, I could

blatantly hear Roc saying, "Flukey! Flukey…
Flukey… Flukey!"

I was trying my best to ignore his
comical behavior, but one of the women told
me that she thought someone was trying to get
my attention.

"Oh, don't worry about him. He's just a
little unbalanced and kinda strange," I replied.
"Is it okay for me to have a seat?"

"Sure," they said in unison.

I sat down and said thanks to both
women for the drink.

"You're welcome. It was our pleasure."

I then introduced myself. In return, the
beautiful ladies also introduced themselves as
Valentina and Alisha.

Valentina asked, "Haven't we seen you
here before?"

"I'm not sure. I don't really get out too
often."

She smiled and said, "I think you may
know my friend Maria."

"Did you say Maria? I can't be sure; I'd
have to see her face to remember."

Alisha chimed in, "Don't they call you
by another name?"

"Well, that might depend on who you
ask."

Valentina continued, "Don't they call
you Thunder Pipe Mike?"

Principles

I laughed as I replied, "*Now* I remember your friend Maria. She told you about that, huh?"

"Yep, and she showed me pictures of you, too," she laughed.

"Okay, guilty as charged," I said with a smirk.

"I told Alisha that I thought it was you."

Alisha then asked me, "So, what brought you out of the house tonight?"

"I'm just here with some family unwinding from a busy week."

"Well, our week is just beginning. Alisha's birthday is in a few weeks, but we're celebrating all month long."

"Perfect... I'm having a birthday party in a couple of weeks."

"Are we invited?" they both asked.

I told them, "Absolutely. You can be my guests of honor, but I hope I don't have to wait a couple of weeks to spend more time with you ladies."

Alisha said, "No we won't make you wait that long."

"You know I'm going to hold you to that."

"I want you to."

"Mike, I think we should dance," Valentina flirted.

"Do you like dancing?" Alisha added.

"Not really, but I will if you two are dancing with me."

"Okay, let's dance then…"

The ladies jumped out of their seats, grabbed my hands, and pulled me to the dance floor. We danced off and on for a while and had a few more drinks. During one of the moments when we were sitting down taking a break from dancing, Valentina asked me if she could ask a personal question.

"Sure, I don't mind at all," I replied.

She asked if I had any sexual fantasies.

"Yeah, of course, I do, but can I be absolutely honest with you?"

"Yes… You said that you'd be honest with me."

I told Valentina that I have quite a few sexual fantasies, but tonight I'm fantasizing about having two beautiful women leaving the club with me, going back to my place, and having a night of incredibly nasty, wild passionate sex.

Both ladies smiled and said, "Okay, let's go."

"Ooooo weeeee mane! Give me a few minutes so I can take care of the tab for my family. Meet me in front of the club."

Valentina replied, "Sounds good to me, Papi," as they headed towards the exit.

I went to the bar and paid the tab. Then, I texted Roc and told him that the girls and I were leaving and to let Nick and Ale know. When I made it to the front entrance, Valentina and Alisha followed me to the car, and then we headed to my house. Once we got inside, I locked the front door and walked upstairs. They followed me. I went into the bathroom and turned on the shower. Meanwhile, Valentina started unbuttoning my shirt while Alisha was taking off my shoes and pants. I began undressing them as fast as they were undressing me.

Now that we were all naked, I opened the steamy shower door and walked inside. Both ladies followed right behind me. Valentina began kissing and licking on my chest and neck while Alisha rubbed my back and slid her warm wet tongue between my shoulder blades. After spending some time in the shower, we continued our escapade on the balcony. I'm almost certain my neighbors heard Valentina making loud noises as I pulled her hair while savagely fucking her from behind.

She screamed, "Oh! Oh! Oh, Mike! Oh, goddamn, Papi!"

While I was fucking Valentina, Alisha licked my earlobes and kissed my neck. The three of us eventually made it into my bedroom where the hot passionate sex continued. I laid Alisha across my mattress, spread her legs apart, and began slowly stroking the inside of her body. Valentina was softly kissing her on the inner thighs as I continued to stroke her wet vagina. Alisha took my right hand and placed it around her throat.

Principles

I began to gradually apply pressure while gently squeezing her titties with my left hand. The three of us endlessly continued having lustful, intense sex until we exhausted ourselves and fell asleep. I'm not even sure what time it was when we finished.

The next morning I was awakened by my phone ringing. It was Roc checking up on me, trying to see if I was okay. I told him that I was fine and that I had to handle something real quick but would call him back later.

"Cool," he said.

"Aye, Roc, thanks for checking up on me though. I appreciate it," I said as I eased out of the bed with the ladies and went to the bathroom.

"No problem, Flukey."

I took a long sigh and said, "Really, Roc? Oh yeah… By the way, that little bullshit at the lounge last night was uncalled for."

He laughed and said, "What? Ain't that what yo mom and pops called you when you were a kid?"

"My point exactly. You're the only person who still calls me that. They even stopped at some point."

"Why you being sensitive? All in your feelings and shit this morning…"

"I'm not."

"Yeah you are, bruh," he argued.

"Aight man, I'll talk to you later."

"Okay, bye Flukey," he teased and hung up the phone.

I was still holding the phone but laughing at Roc's antics at the same time. I walked back into the bedroom to wake Valentina and Alisha. I told them that I had somewhere to be shortly and that I could have an Uber on the way to pick them up. They agreed. While I got myself together, both women decided to lay around a little while longer, but they eventually got up and got dressed. Meanwhile, I went into the kitchen to make coffee for them. It seemed like as soon as I poured our coffee and sat down at the kitchen table, the Uber driver called my phone to say that he was outside.

"Well, ladies, your ride is here."

"When will we get together again?" they asked.

I reached for Valentina's cell phone, typed my number in, and told her to call me. Alisha then handed me her phone, and I typed my number there also. Then, they both kissed me on the lips and left. Now, I know you're probably thinking, "*Mike, what happened to the lesson?*" That was just a fucking sexcapade. There's no lesson in that. I said that teamwork made the dream work. Well, didn't their teamwork make the dream work? Lesson learned.

Lesson 2: Time

One time I read a quote by Miles Davis that says, "Time isn't the main thing. It's the *only* thing." Time may not seem that important to most people, but once it's gone, we can never get it back. God only gives us twenty-four hours in a day. To a lazy muthafucka this just means that they have twelve hours to sleep and twelve hours to bullshit. To a hustler, we're thinking about how we can maximize the twenty-four hours we're given because we look at time differently. We all know that time is money, but time is also used to set life and death events. Like any ordinary day going by, there's a beginning, middle, and end. Certain events have to take place at certain times to create certain outcomes. Time is precious; therefore, it's not ours to waste.

I'm up most mornings between the hours of 4:00 a.m. and 5:30 a.m. No, I don't have a sleeping disorder, and I'm not an insomniac. It's just that my mind never stops thinking. I'm always thinking about the decisions I've made in my past. Like most people, I often wonder if I could have handled certain situations differently or if I did the right thing. I know there's nothing I can do about it now, but I still sometimes lie in bed looking at the ceiling and wondering what if. There's no magic time capsule that allows us to go back and fix our fuck-ups. Whether we like it or not

Principles

sometimes our past can dictate our future.
That's why we have to use our time wisely and
make the right decisions the first time. Once
that time is gone, it's not coming back.

Lesson 3:
Trust No One

I've created a few businesses and investments to clean my dirty money. These businesses also serve as exit plans from the drug game. The fact of the matter is that no one can do this shit forever. If you try to make slanging dope a career, there are only two ways out – either jail or death. I don't care who you are; those are your only options in this game. You have to get in, make your money, invest your money, and get out. The drug business is a dirty game. People will turn on you. They'll even turn others against you for strategic gains. You have to be cautious about the people that you're around and the people that surround them. I've come to realize that everyone doesn't have the same code of morality, and I have to be careful with that. People are who they are, and there's no changing that.

I've come a long way. I've seen a lot, and I've learned a lot. I know that just because you'll take a bullet for someone doesn't mean that they'll take that same bullet for you. You can tell yourself they will, but you'll never really know unless time and opportunity present themselves. This game is full of trial and error. That's why I'm just extremely cautious of some people. I'd like to think that

Principles

I'm a pretty good judge of character, but
sometimes I can be wrong. I'll never come off
to a person as negative or disrespectful because
that's just not who I am. I wasn't raised like
that. I can give almost anyone the benefit of the
doubt. Hell, I'll somewhat trust you until you
show me otherwise. And, I'll give you just
enough rope to hang yourself if need be.

Lesson 4:
Communication

Communication is the key to any relationship whether it's business or personal. There's a local coffee shop a couple of blocks away from my home. I usually go there maybe three or four times a week because I like the peaceful atmosphere. While I was sitting at the table enjoying my coffee one day, I glanced up for just a quick second to look out the window. I noticed a lady named Katrina Lee crossing the street walking towards the coffee shop. Katrina's one of my main business partners. She and I have been working with each other for years, and we have a beautiful relationship. I've helped Katrina open four separate businesses. We have a beauty salon, a nail shop, a day spa for women, and a day spa for men. In return, she runs my drug money through the businesses to make it look like clean cash.

We did have somewhat of a relationship for a short time, but I knew I wasn't ready for the level of commitment she deserves. I didn't want to damage her emotionally, so I gracefully bowed out. She's a wonderful woman, and she's about her business. Katrina has it all. She's beautiful, intelligent, attractive, and most of all, we communicate well together. I just need to get my shit together to be the man she needs to love her right. Until then, we'll just keep our beautiful business relationship intact.

As soon as Katrina entered the coffee shop's front door, she came to sit down by me.

"Who you waiting for? One of your women?" she asked before her sexy ass even hit the seat.

"Well, I guess I was just waiting for you to come and bless me with your presence."

"Okay, but if you are waiting for someone, she needs to find another table because I have something important to talk about," she replied.

"So, just to be clear, you're saying that you need to find another table?"

"You know what I mean," she playfully snapped.

I laughed and properly greeted her. "Well, anyway… Good morning, Katrina. Would you like a coffee or anything?"

"Good morning, and no, I would not."

"Do I sense an attitude this morning?" I asked.

Katrina immediately asked me why she wasn't invited to the club last night. I told her that it was just me and the guys and I didn't think she would want to come.

"Ummmm hmmm… Next time, let me make that decision, Mike."

"Okay, Katrina. So, what's up? I never see you this early in the morning."

"I figured you'd be here, so I decided to stop by."

"Okay, so now what, Beautiful? Are we having any problems with the businesses?"

Katrina told me that the businesses are fine, but that a Haitian or Jamaican-sounding guy came into the spa asking a lot of questions about me.

"Did he come in for service or just to ask questions?"

"He did come in for service, but he had too many questions for my liking."

"That's probably just another nosy muthafucka trying to see how we getting it. It's nothing to worry about. You know when you're making money, curiosity and envy come with that."

"Look, Mike… I've been around long enough to know when to be concerned and when not to be concerned about something. The guy was talking loudly, and I heard him mention the name Michael Davis to the other guys in the steam room. The guy was saying that within a few weeks Michael Davis would be finished, and within three months he would have your entire operation. I needed to see what this guy looked like, so I knocked on the steam room door, walked inside, and asked if they needed any more towels. The guy said, 'No, not right now.' I needed to make sure I matched the Jamaican's accent with a face, so I asked a second time if they were sure they didn't need anything. The guy replied, 'Isn't no the same in every language?"

Katrina said that something just didn't feel right about him. When she purposely made eye contact with the guy, his eyes had an oddly menacing look - almost like death. She said that his eyes looked dark, evil, and soulless as if nothing was there.

"He scared the hell out of me, Mike. After the guy and his crew left, I checked the sign-in book."

I asked her, "So what did you find out?"

"The guy signed in under the name Jean–Jacques. I tried searching the internet for any information under that name but came up with nothing."

"I need you to check with all our contacts in New York, Atlanta, Los Angeles, and here in Texas. Find out anything you can about this Jean-Jacques."

"I've already been asking around for you. Jean–Jacques is his birth name, but on the streets, he goes by Richblood. He's originally from Port Royal, Jamaica but he's been here in the states for six or seven years. RichBlood's family runs almost 95% of all the drug shipments coming in or out of the Caribbean Islands. His organization runs deep. They have control in Haiti, Jamaica, Tobago, and Trinidad.

"Even though his family is here in The States, he's still able to maintain control in the

Caribbean. RichBlood uses his family or business associates to carry out hits on anyone that gets in his way. His methods of murder can get brutal and gruesome. He likes to send messages of intimidation. He's been known to skin people alive, cut out tongues and eyes, and dismember limbs then send the body parts to unsuspecting family members. Mike, this guy is no fucking joke, and I'm not sure how much Richblood knows about us or our organization."

I said, "I don't know what Richblood's angle is, but he could be here trying to expand his operation. If that's the case, I'm the only thing standing in his way."

"Look, I need you to watch your back and to be careful. You need to keep your head on a swivel. If this dude continues asking around for you, it's just a matter of time before he finds you."

"It's like I told you earlier," I replied. "There's nothing to worry about. I'll find Richblood long before he finds me. Continue business as normal, but I want you to stay strapped at all times. In the meantime, I'll have some of the guys keep an extra eye out for you and the businesses. Just in case this nigga decides to try some dumb shit, we'll be ready."

Lesson 5:
Warning Before Destruction

Most of the time there's always calm before the storm. Some people play it safe and pay attention to the warning while others take chances and gamble with their lives. I had to see RichBlood. I needed some understanding, but most of all, I had to let that muthafucka know that he's not the only shooter in town. I called my circle and let everybody know the play just in case shit went left. After I explained the situation, I made it absolutely clear to everyone that I wanted them to chill and let me see what dude had up. Then, I called Nick to get a location on Richblood. I found out that he has a mansion on the Northside of town, and I couldn't wait to pay him a visit.

Once I arrived at the mansion, I parked along the street completely out of view. I exited my vehicle and walked towards the right side of Richblood's mansion and slowly made my way to the left side of the home trying to analyze my surroundings. I noticed that the exterior of the home was guarded by five security agents and a few cameras. I needed to gain access to the inside. I waited patiently to catch just one of the guards slipping. I didn't have to wait too long. I heard the patio door slide open, and then one of the security guards walked out towards the swimming pool. He lit a cigarette and walked further away from the patio towards the back fence near the end of the property. I knew this was my chance.

While the guard's back was turned, I casually walked through the patio door and snuck my way upstairs to Richblood's office. Once I was inside the office, I slid on a pair of gloves and started looking around trying to see if there was any evidence or a clue as to what he had planned. I found a few family photos and a pistol behind the desk. I removed the clip of bullets from the gun and returned it behind the desk. Then, I sat in a chair that was placed in a dark remote part of the office and quietly waited for Richblood to come home.

When he finally arrived, he opened the office door and walked inside. As soon as he turned on the office lights and saw me sitting unexpectedly in the chair, I could easily tell that he was startled by my presence.

"Mr. Davis, I see your reputation precedes you. Of course, I wasn't expecting to see you so soon."

"Well, RichBlood, I'm a very busy man, and I don't like to keep people waiting."

"How you were able to get past my security and make it up here?"

"It wasn't too difficult... Just perfect timing."

"Would you like a drink? Maybe rum, scotch, or whatever your flavor is," he offered.

Principles

"All bullshit aside... I'd much rather get straight to the point, RichBlood. Why have you been looking for me? What do you want?"

"Honestly, I had intentions of killing you, but I recently did a little more checking into your background. However, I admire your hustle and prefer to do business with you instead. I've been moving weight for a long time, and I know all the major players in the game. By far, you're one of the best."

I sat in his chair listening without interrupting.

"Mr. Davis, I like you because you move in silence. You're like a phantom of sorts. I feel like you'd much rather be heard of than seen, and to me, that's a noble thing. Most people in this business don't have your level of skill or intelligence."

RichBlood then tells me that I'm a formidable adversary but quite possibly an even better ally, and he wants to become friends and not enemies.

"I'm absolutely satisfied with the way things are going, and I'm not particularly interested in making any new business partners, friends, or associates. If that's what all this is about, you're wasting both of our time."

He took a short pause, then he asked me if I had ever faced rejection. He then went on to tell me that for some people rejection can cause mental and physical pain - so much pain, in

36

fact, that it makes people give up. Even if the pain doesn't kill that person, it stops them from ever trying again.

"Mr. Davis, I'm a different type of person. See, people like me use that pain and rejection to channel anger and frustration to grow stronger. Once I'm stronger than the one who inflicted my pain, I tend to just take what I want, how I want it, and when I want it."

I replied, "You do realize that taking something from someone without asking is considered stealing. In some places, the consequence for stealing is usually death."

"Is that a threat, Mr. Davis?"

"No not a threat, RichBlood… See, a threat may cause damage. I can promise you, I *will* cause damage. I continued, "A gorilla will always pound his chest as a warning before he attacks."

I stood up and began walking toward the office door. Just before reaching for the door handle, I turned to look him directly in his eyes.

"Consider this your only warning, Richblood."

As I walked down the hallway I could hear him throwing things around his office in anger. Just before departing the mansion, I handed someone on the security staff RichBlood's gun clip.

"Do me a favor and make sure you give this back to ya boy for me."

Lesson 6:
Never Get Too Comfortable

It was 11:30 p.m., and I was sitting in bed watching television when my cell phone rang. It was Alejandro calling. He told me that three of our corner boys had been badly beaten, tortured, and shot execution-style. I immediately sat up and moved to the edge of my bed.

"Are you fucking kidding me? Where were the bodies found?"

"They were dumped in a field on the eastside," he replied calmly.

"Who do we have controlling the territory on the eastside?"

"The Ben Lejos gang and their leader Chinx are running the eastside."

I was asking Alejandro these questions, but in the back of my mind, I was wondering if Richblood had anything to do with this.

"My next question is very important, Ale. Are the bodies missing anything like limbs, eyes, or anything else?"

He told me that he didn't think so, but he wasn't sure.

"Make sure, and then call me back because your answer will determine my next move. Aye, and don't mention this conversation to anyone just yet."

Ale said, "I gotcha, Boss."

Principles

While I waited for verification from Alejandro, I called Katrina to make sure she was okay, but there was no answer. I texted Roc and asked him to go by and check on her and then meet me at the warehouse in one hour. We both arrived about the same time. As we approached the entrance, I asked if Katrina was okay.

"She was still half asleep when she came to the door, but she was fine. What's going on, Flukey? Did something happen that I need to know about?"

I told Roc that someone had killed three of our corner boys and that I had Ale checking on some things before we made any moves on anyone.

"Damn, do you think it was that muthafucka RichBlood?"

"I'm not sure yet, but we'll most definitely find out. If it was RichBlood, he's going to pay for this with his own life."

Meanwhile, Ale called me back with some unexpected news. He said that the bodies were in bad shape but not disfigured. This threw me for a loop. Now I wasn't sure who could have killed my corner boys.

Ale asked me, "What's the next move, boss?"

"Meet me and Roc on the eastside. We need to locate Chinx and ask him a few questions," I replied.

Principles

Then, I made a couple of phone calls and found out that Chinx was at the Dancing Dolls strip club. So we headed there. I told Roc and Ale that Chinx would be surrounded by his clique of Ben Lejos.

I said, "If shit goes left, shoot up everything in the muthafucking club, that's the only way we'll make it back out alive."

Roc, Ale, and I entered the club through a back door. I spotted Chinx in the lounge area. He was sitting in a private section with nine or ten of his guys. There were at least another fifteen or twenty of his men scattered around the club. As I approached Chinx, one of his men raised his hand towards me and grabbed the gun around his waist.

"Who the fuck are you, bro?" he asked.

I looked him in his eyes and said, "I can be a gift or a curse, but you got five seconds to decide."

Chinx chimed in. "That's the homie. Let him through, bro." As I proceeded towards Chinx, he said, "I apologize about my boy Don Neto. He goes from zero to one hundred real quick."

"Well, you might need to handle yo boy cause shit like dat can get you killed real quick too."

Don Neto was giving me a cold-hearted, fucked up stare the entire time I was talking to Chinx, and I was giving him the same fucked up stare right back.

Principles

"Have a seat," Chinx said. "Damn, Mike, this must be some real shit. I hardly ever see you on the eastside. Plus, you're at a strip club of all places."

"I'm not here for small talk, Chinx. I'm here about business. I need to ask you some very important questions. If you lie to me, we'll kill everybody in this muthafucka including you, and you know we don't miss."

Chinx leaned forward and rested his elbows on his knees. "Okay, big dog, you got my attention."

"Three of my soldiers got killed tonight night. You wouldn't by chance know anything about that, would you?"

"Hell no, Mike. I'm not fucking crazy! I mean I heard about it, but I would never in a million years do no stupid shit like that. I got mad respect for you bro."

I asked, "How do I know you're not lying to me, Chinx? Tell me why in fuck should I believe a word you're saying right now?"

"I would never lie to you, Mike. I can remember when I didn't have shit; it was you who put me on and gave me a chance when no one else would. I'll always be grateful for that. I consider you family, Mike."

"I have a second question," I continued. "I need you to explain to me why my guys were found dead on the eastside in your territory."

"Look, man, I don't know, but I can ask around."

"Have you seen anything or anyone unusual in the last couple of weeks or days?"

"Nah, not really Mike... Well, wait a minute.... There was a black SS Camaro passing by one of the trap houses on Lake Street this week. I remember because the first time it passed, they drove by really slowly. The passenger let his window down and started mean-mugging me, so I hit his ass up with the Ben Lejos sign."

Chinx demonstrated the sign as if he was reenacting the moment.

"The second time they came through, the Camaro stopped, so I grabbed my strap and walked towards the car but then the driver smashed off. At some point later that night when I left the trap house headed home, I made a quick stop by a convenience store to get some cigars to roll with. As I walked out of the store, I noticed the same black Camaro from earlier that day parked on the other side of the parking lot. I got back in my car and drove off."

He steered his hands as if he was gripping the steering wheel in his car.

"Every right turn I made, they made. Every left turn I made, they made. I knew I was being followed, so I sped up just enough to get briefly out of sight. Then, I quickly pulled into a dark alley and turned off my car lights. I managed to lose whoever it was, but I stayed parked in the ally for ten or fifteen minutes before I tried heading home again."

I asked Chinx did he get a good look at anyone in the car that night.

"No, the windows were tinted too dark to see anything inside the car."

"You had mentioned earlier that the car passed by the trap driving slow with the passenger window down. Did you see anything then?"

"I still couldn't see the driver, but the passenger was wearing dark shades and dreads."

"So he had dreads?"

"Yeah dreads, and he looked kinda Jamaican, Rastafarian, or some shit."

As Chinx was talking, I knew Ale and Roc had to be thinking the same thing that I was thinking.

"As a matter of fact, when the car stopped and smashed off again, I noticed a sticker of a Jamaican flag on the back window."

To me it just seemed like the more Chinx spoke, the more his words implicated Richblood.

"I'm telling you, Mike. Something's strange about those muthafuckas."

"I'll check it out and get back with you," I replied. "In the meantime, let me know if you hear anything else or if you see the black Camaro again."

"Bet, and if you need anything let me know."

I told Chinx, "Keep your phone close because I just might need you."

"You got it, Mike."

We shook hands and did a one-sided embrace and then Ale, Roc, and I went out through the back door again to exit the club. As we approached our cars, I saw a black Camaro parked in the shadows, but I couldn't tell if anyone was sitting inside. I guess my demeanor changed when I saw it because Roc asked me, "What's wrong, Flukey?"

I told him and Ale, "Don't look right now, but I think I see a black Camaro. I'm not sure if it's the same Camaro Chinx was just talking about though."

Roc quickly replied, "Let's run up on that muthafucka and find out."

I told Roc, "Nah, let's just play it cool. Don't look. Just keep walking."

Ale's car was parked right behind the Camaro. I asked him if he still had his bullet-proof vest on.

"Hell yeah," he replied.

"Alright... Walk to your car and look for a Jamaican flag on the back window of the Camaro. Also, try to see if the car's occupied. If anyone's in the car, I want you to signal me, and I'll handle it from there."

Principles

"No problem," he replied as he walked to his car.

Roc and I were standing next to my car talking but also watching and paying close attention to Ale. As he approached his car, I could see the passenger's window on the Camaro slowly begin to roll down. I knew for certain that someone is inside the Camaro at that point. Not knowing what to expect next, I was getting nervous and hoping Ale was cautious. The passenger flicked a cigarette out the window and almost simultaneously opened the passenger door to exit the vehicle. Before I could holler and warn Ale, the passenger pulled out an assault rifle and released a gang of bullets in Ale's direction.

Ale ran toward his vehicle for cover as shots whisked by his body barely missing him. Roc, Ale, and I returned gunfire hitting the passenger in the leg and hitting the Camaro several times. After a brief shootout, the passenger was somehow able to return to the Camaro. The driver pulled him inside the car and sped off. I felt like this could have been a setup. I told Ale that I wanted him to stay at the club and make sure Chinx didn't try to leave. Then, I grabbed my car keys out of my jacket pocket, and Roc and I took off in my car. We chased the Camaro through the late-night city streets. During the pursuit, we quickly reached speeds over one hundred miles per hour, running traffic light after traffic light.

Principles

I knew the SS Camaro couldn't outrun my 6.4-liter Dodge Challenger. With every corner they turned, we were right on their asses. They merged onto the interstate, and we were now exceeding 130 mph. Roc and I were quickly gaining on the Camaro.

As I stuck close behind them, I told Roc "Get ready to light their asses up."

I was trying to get close as possible to the driver's side, but the driver kept aggressively switching from lane to lane blocking me. Once I finally got an opening, I floored my Dodge. In a matter of seconds, we were side by side with the Camaro.

I hollered, "Now Roc!"

And, he immediately started shooting his assault rifle, rapidly firing shot after shot into the driver's side of the car. The bullets were ripping holes through the Camaro's cabin and interior. The driver finally lost control of the car and hit a guardrail, sending the car flipping several times before finally coming to a rest on its caved-in roof. I parked my car, grabbed my gun, and walked toward the mangled car. I wanted to see who we had been chasing. I wanted to know who'd sent them to kill my family and me. I wanted to know if these were the same people responsible for killing my corner boys. More importantly, I wanted to know if all this shit would lead back to Chinx, RichBlood, or both of them.

Principles

When I approached the damaged car, I could see the driver's motionless body lying face-up on the pavement. He looked to be black or of Jamaican descent, but there was no way I could be sure without hearing him speak. I kneeled by the driver and noticed that the driver had a very distinctive tattoo on his neck. I asked Roc to look and see if the tattoo looked familiar to him. He said that he didn't recognize it, but I was almost certain that I had seen that tattoo before; I just couldn't remember when or where. While I was still kneeling by the driver of the Camaro, I realized that the passenger was still moving.

"Roc, take a picture of his tat so I can send it to Nick. Then, check his pockets to see if you can find something useful, and I'll check the passenger."

Once I got face to face with the passenger I could tell that he was badly injured during the car crash. I also noticed that he had the same tattoo on his neck as the driver. I kneeled next to him to get a closer look. As I watched his body gasp for oxygen over and over again, I explained to him that he was losing a lot of blood.

"If you don't get some help soon, you're not going to make it," I said. "I can get you some help and have an ambulance on the way in a matter of seconds, but first I need you to tell me who sent you."

Principles

The man stared me in the face and began laughing.

"I'm going to ask you one last time. Who was it that sent you?"

"You're a dead mon," he said as he spit blood on the pavement. "There is no bitch in me, Chi-Chi mon. I tell you nothing. I wish to die first."

I shook my head, stood over him, and said, "Okay, well you got your wish."

Then, I shot him two times in the head and once in the chest. I just stood there for a second to watch that piece of shit take his last breath.

Roc's voice interrupted my thoughts. "Hey, Flukey, we need to hurry up and leave before the cops come."

"Yeah, let's go because now we got a fucking war on our hands, and we need to make preparations."

Roc and I got back into my car and drove off into the night.

Lesson 7:
Never Burn Bridges

When I was a kid, one of my aunties used to tell me to be careful how I treat others when they're down because eventually everyone gets a turn. In other words, you could be on and popping one day and lose it all the next. That same auntie also told me to never burn my bridges. I asked her what she meant by that. She told that someone that is of no value to you right now could be of value to you later in life, so be sure to maintain a good relationship with them. That little piece of wisdom stuck with me.

The next morning after the high-speed chase, I called my boy Nick that works at the DEA's office. I asked him if he could do me a favor and check on something for me.

"I gotcha, big dog. What do you need?"

"Look at the picture I just texted of a tattoo and see if you can identify it," I asked.

"That shouldn't be a problem. I can just search the database and let you know something shortly."

I said, "Thanks, Nick."

While I waited for him to get back to me, I decided to go check on Katrina and the business. I called her to see where she was, and she told me that she was at the salon. She said that she was just about to call me regarding something important.

"Don't move. I'll be there in a few minutes," I said.

As soon as I walked into the salon, Katrina grabbed my hand and pulled me to a room in the back away from customers. She told me she had been noticing money coming up missing from the cash drawers.

"How much money, and why in the fuck I'm just hearing about this?"

"I didn't worry about it at first because it was small amounts like forty dollars or fifty dollars here and there. But, this morning when I checked, we were short like a thousand dollars."

I said, "Okay, let's just add a few more cameras, replace the money, and move it to another spot."

"But that's not all," she replied. "When I went by the warehouse to get more product, I noticed a couple of cases were missing."

"When you say a couple, you do mean just two right?"

"Yes, Mike, it was two cases."

"Are you sure only two cases were missing?"

"Yes, nigga. I can count!"

Katrina reassured me that it was just two because she had done her usual count of the product for the fourth time this week.

She said, "We're missing a case of Oxycodone and one case of Codeine."

" Don't mention this to anyone else until we figure this out. Do you think someone could have followed you to the warehouse?" I asked.

"I don't think so, but anything's possible."

"Can we use one of the computers here at the salon to look at camera footage of the warehouse?" I asked.

"Yeah, I'm sure we can. Give me a second."

In no time at all, she had the camera system up and ready to view.

"Pull up the warehouse parking lot and street footage around the warehouse. How long does the camera footage date back?"

"The cameras can go back two or three months," she replied.

"Whoever did it had to have known that we don't have cameras inside the warehouse." Katrina pulled up the footage, and the first thing we noticed was a white SUV parked across the street from the warehouse. A female dressed in a black hoodie got out of it and walked across the street toward the warehouse. The camera footage showed her entering the building through a side window and exiting out through the same side window ten minutes later with the two cases of product. The lady then ran back across the street to the SUV and drove away.

I said, "First a fucking war, and now this shit."

"A war?"

"Don't worry about it, Katrina. I'll explain it to you later. Right now we need to find out who this woman is ASAP."

"I'll get right on it," she said as she logged off and we headed back toward the front of the salon.

While I was walking back to my car, Nick called me with information on the tattoos. He said that he traced the tattoo images back to a Jamaican gang called the Posse Boyz that is run by Jean-Jacques.

"Just as I had thought. I suspected Richblood all along, but now I have proof. I may need some backup. Can you pull some strings and get me visitation inside the Angola State Penitentiary?"

"How soon?" Nick asked.

"Tonight if possible, no matter the cost.

"Okay, I'll set it up."

***

Later that evening, I was at Angola State Penitentiary. I hadn't seen the inside of that place in a couple of years or so. The person I came to see finally came into the waiting room and took a seat.

"It's been a long time, kid."

I said, "Yeah it has, Uncle Jimmy."

"I really appreciate everything you've been doing for me, nephew. That attorney you hired is the shit. She said that shit's looking real good for me and that I should be home soon."

I told Uncle Jimmy, "Don't worry about it, Unc. That's the least I can do for you."

"So, how's everything been going?"

"Everything's been good, Unc. No complaints here."

"Everything's been good, huh? Nephew the last time you came to see me in person, you had an issue, right?"

I said, "Yeah, you're right, Unc."

"So here we are again probably with another issue that you ain't told me about yet."

"I was working my way to it," I said.

"Well, let's get to it then."

I kinda laughed and said, "I could always fool my pops, but I could never fool you, Unc."

"Boy, you wasn't fooling yo pops. He just made you think that shit. Yo pops is a smart man, Mike. How has he been anyway?"

I replied, "He's been good. I talked to him just the other day."

"Okay enough of the small talk. Let's get to the business."

I told Unc, "There's this Jamaican crew called the Posse Boyz that's run by this muthafucka named Jean-Jacques. He goes by RichBlood. He's been trying to take over my operation by eliminating me and my team. This muthafucka executed three of my corner boys, and he tried to kill one of my top Ben Lejos. This son of a bitch even came after me, Roc and Ale. I can't predict Richblood's next move, but I know that I have to be ready for whatever."

"Yeahhhh, kid you got yo self in some bullshit this time. I mean deep do-do. Dem Jamaicans some crazy muthafuckas," Unc replied. "The first thing you need to do is get you some soldiers together. The second thing you need to do is come up with a plan, and the third thing you need to do is put an end to his ass and those little Pussy Boyz."

"That's why I'm here. My team and organization are built for finesse, not war. I think I may have a way to take down Richblood and his Posse Boyz without having a war. But, just in case my plan doesn't work, I'll need you and the C.G. Mafia for backup. Unc, I just need to know that if me and my crew can't handle these muthafuckas, I can depend on you to help me take they asses out."

Uncle Jimmy replied, "Okay nephew. I know you got this covered like a rug, but if you need me I'm always here for you. You just like me and yo pops kid. If you do that shit right, that Jamaican muthafucka ain't gon know what hit him."

"Thanks, Unc. You always come through for me."

"Don't worry about it kid we family. We always come through for each other, and we always gotta look out for each other no matter what."

"You're right."

Uncle Jimmy stood up. "Now, I need to get back in here, and you need to get back to Texas and figure some shit out." He walked to the door, turned around, and said, "And, next time you come down here, bring me a big booty stripper or something."

We both laughed about it as he walked out the door and back toward his cell. Once I had made it back to my car, I checked my cell phone and realized that I had several missed calls from Katrina. I immediately returned her call. She informed me that she had figured out the identity of the woman that broke into the warehouse and stole our product.

"So, who is it?"

"You're not going to like this, but the woman's name is Madeleine Noriega. I hired Madeleine four months ago to work at the salon."

"Did you do any kind of background check before you hired her?" I asked.

"I did do a background check, and everything came back clean."

"Do you know where she is right now?" I asked.

Principles

"She's still at the salon. Her shop station is the one closest to the front door."

"I'm on the way to the airport. I'll be there in an hour, but I need you to keep an eye on Madeleine for me. Keep her ass on the clock and make sure she doesn't leave the salon."

Lesson 8:
Fear is Forced While
Respect is Earned

When I arrived at the salon, I entered through the front door so I could purposely walk past Madeleine's station. I wanted to see her facial reaction when I passed by. I focused all my attention on her, and we made eye contact for a brief second. She didn't give me the look or the cold stare of a deceitful thief. Instead, Madeleine's demeanor was more like a scared, timid little child. I asked Katrina to follow me to the back office and close the door behind her. Then, I told her that I think someone's making Madeleine do the shit she's doing.

"Why do you think that?" Katrina asked.

"The eyes are the windows to the soul. When I stared at Madeleine, the way she looked at me told me that she's not used to that life. I think she's just trying to survive something or someone. Go get her and bring her back here."

When Madeleine walked inside the office with Katrina I said, "Please have a seat. Do you have any idea why I wanted to see you?"

"No sir. I don't have a clue," she replied nervously.

"I think you know exactly why I wanted to speak to you. Madeleine, I'll get straight to the point. Someone's been stealing money from the salon, but that's not the big problem. The big problem is that a few nights ago someone broke into my warehouse and stole some things from me."

Madeleine responded, "I'm sorry to hear that, Mr. Davis, but what does that have to do with me?"

"Well, nothing if you're honest with me and tell me what I need to know. On the other hand, it could have everything to do with you if I find out that you're lying to me. I truly believe you're a good person that wants to do the right thing. Madeleine, I'm going to ask you one time and one time only. Who's making you steal from me and why?"

She had a look of confusion and fear on her face. "I don't know what you're talking about, Mr. Davis."

I pulled a gun from my waist and placed it on top of the desk. "Are you sure? Madeleine, I want you to understand that I don't have a problem with killing you. I really don't, but I know that's not for you or me. All you gotta do is tell me what I need to know, and I'll let you live. You can walk away. It's your decision, but you better choose wisely."

Madeleine put her head down and started crying. "I didn't want to do it, but he made me. He said that he would kill me and my daughter if I didn't do what he asked."

I asked, "Who are you talking about? Who threatened you and your daughter?"

"His name is Richblood."

Katrina and I looked at each other. "How do you know him?"

"I don't know him. A few weeks ago, he approached me while I was leaving the salon. He called me by name and asked me if I wanted to make some extra cash. I told him no thanks and continued to walk away. That's when RichBlood grabbed my arm, pulled me close to him, and told me that he had my daughter Brittany. He said that he was sure Brittany would be very disappointed if he told her that her mother didn't want to cooperate and could have saved her life but chose otherwise. That's when I dropped everything and froze. He told me that he was now my master and puppeteer that would be pulling all the strings.

"I asked him what he did with my daughter, and he said she was in a safe place and would remain safe and unharmed as long as I followed his instructions. He told me that if I refused to cooperate, he would make a call and have Brittany decapitated, cut up, and discarded like a dog. I took a deep breath and asked Richblood what he wanted me to do. He walked me to his car so we could talk privately. He said he needed someone within my network that could help him infiltrate and sabotage the organization. He told me that time was of the essence, and as an incentive, every day I don't provide useful information, I'll have to pay him to keep my daughter alive and safe."

I asked Madeleine, "So that's why you were stealing from me?"

"Yes. I didn't know what else to do. So, the other day I followed Katrina to a warehouse. I watched her go inside and come back out with some boxes. After she left, I went inside the building and that's when I found all the drugs. I had to pay Richblood in either money or drugs. There was so much that I didn't think anyone would miss a few boxes here and there."

I asked Madeleine, "Was Richblood ever curious about where you were getting the product to give to him?"

Madeleine said, "No, but I'm sure he probably had an idea. Plus, I never gave anything directly to RichBlood. He told me to give everything to Don Neto."

"Don Neto!?" I replied.

My mind instantly flashed back to that night at the strip club. At the time, I didn't know who Don Neto was, but he knew exactly who I was. That muthafucka had been working with Richblood all along just watching and plotting the entire fucking time.

Principles

"Have you ever met or heard of a guy by the name of Chinx?"

Madeleine said, "No, just Don Neto." She told me that her first assignment was to meet up with Don Neto and get his contact information. Then, she would have to call or text him to keep him informed of my whereabouts whenever possible. When the time was right, Don Neto would eventually kill me.

"Okay, Madeleine. Now I understand why you did it, but that still doesn't make shit right. I can return your daughter safe and sound, but you're going to have to help me do that. If you do exactly what I ask you to do, by the time RichBlood figures anything out, you'll already have your daughter back in your arms."

Katrina added, "Madeleine, this may be your only way to get your daughter back. If I were you, I would accept the offer."

She agreed and then asked me what she needed to do.

"Where can I find Don Neto?"

"I don't know, but he always calls or sends a text to tell me where to meet him."

"So, you never meet at the same place?"

"No, it's always somewhere different," she replied.

"That means that Don Neto has your daughter. Richblood probably has him hiding her somewhere close. That's why he's switching up the meeting spots each time to keep you guessing. I need his cell phone number. Katrina will give you a burner phone. I need you to use the burner to call Don Neto's cell phone at some point," I said as I turned toward Katrina. "Get Roc and Ale on the phone and have them meet me at the warehouse as soon as possible."

I left the ladies in the office to handle the orders I'd just given. On my way to the warehouse, I called Nick and asked him if he could track a cell phone for me.

"Yeah, I gotcha, Mike," he said like always.

I gave him Don Neto's cell number, and I immediately heard Nick typing on his office computer keyboard. A few seconds later, he told me that he was getting a location signal from a house in South Dallas not too far from the salon. He sent me the location, and I told him to let me know if Don Neto's location change.

Ale and Roc made it to the warehouse just minutes before me. They were already inside awaiting my arrival.

"We have business to handle. Mask up, and I'll explain everything on the way." I said as soon as I walked in and saw them standing in position like soldiers.

I called Nick again before arriving at the location just to make sure Don Neto hadn't left.

"Nah, he's still at the same location in south Dallas."

"I need you to run by Chinx's house or find out where he is."

"I can do that, but why?"

"He may be in some deep shit and he doesn't even know it. I just need you to get to him before Richblood does."

Nick said, "Okay, no problem. I'll head by his house first before I go anywhere else."

Ale, Roc, and I slowly drove past the house where Don Neto was and parked a block or so away. Then, I called Madeleine and told her to listen to me very carefully. "I need to know what room inside the house Don Neto will be in. So, in exactly five minutes, I need you to call his cell phone from the burner that Katrina gave you earlier. When Don Neto answers, don't say anything. Just hang up, wait one minute, and call back a second time. Wait another minute and hang up. Then, a third and final time, do the same thing. After you make the third call, wait for me to call you."

Madeleine simply said, "Okay," and hung up the phone.

As Ale, Roc, and I approached the back of the house we waited to hear Don Neto's phone ring. I had Roc go to the left side of the house. I sent Ale to the right side of the house, and I stayed by the back door. Ale told me that he could see Madeleine's daughter Brittany through a small crack in the window blinds.

Principles

She was tied to a chair and blindfolded. Now I just needed Madeleine to call Don Neto's cell phone so we could keep up with his exact location inside the residence and keep him distracted. I wanted to catch Don Neto by surprise.

When Madeleine made the first phone call, I could hear Don Neto's voice but couldn't tell yet where he was exactly. Once she made the second phone call, Roc signaled that he could hear him on the right side of the house. When she made the third call, he was still on the right side of the house. I told Roc and Ale that it was now or never. I kicked in the back door, and we all rushed into the room where Don Neto was. He tried to reach for his gun, but I abruptly shot him in the right shoulder.

"Ahhh, goddamn it! Muthafucka, you shot me! Ahhhhh! You bitch ass muthafuckas! All ya'll dead!"

I said, "Whoa, whoa… Calm down lil bitch. I don't even know why you tripping. You had to know that I was eventually coming for you."

Don Neto said, "I told Richblood he should have killed your ass when he had the chance."

"RichBlood doesn't listen very well. If he would have listened to me, you wouldn't be in the fucked-up position you're in right now. What do you think he was going to do to you after he finished using you? Did you think he was going to put you down and break bread with you? I know that you're not the sharpest tool in the shed, but you had to know that he was going to kill you next."

Don Neto replied, "I'm not afraid to die you Hijo de puta. If you gone kill me, just shut up and kill me."

"Oh don't worry about that my boy. I'm definitely killing your ass right after you tell me what I want to know."

I told Roc and Ale to pick Don Neto up and put him in the chair by the bed.

"Where does Richblood keep his money and product?"

"I'm not telling you shit," he said.

Roc punched him in the face.

"You're making this harder than it has to be." I asked him again, "Where is it, Don Neto?"

He spitted blood from his mouth and said, "I told you I'm not saying shit."

Roc punched him in the face repeatedly for several seconds. I looked on the floor to my left and saw an open bottle of tequila. I asked Ale to hand me the bottle and a lighter. I pulled the cap off the tequila bottle and began pouring it all over Don Neto.

"Last chance, muthafucka. You can cough it up or spit it out."

Don Neto said, "Everything's at a warehouse on 23rd and Milam."

"Now see, Don, that wasn't so difficult, was it."

I told Ale and Roc to help him get up from the chair. Once he was standing I told him, "I need you to help me do one more thing."

"What now?"

"I need you to send a message to RichBlood for me," I said.

Then, I shot Don Neto between the eyes. He fell back against the wooden chair, breaking it into several pieces as his body hit the floor. I left him there and walked into the room where Brittany was. I told Roc to take off her blindfold and untie her hands and feet.

"Brittany, we're here to help you. We're going to get you back home safely to your mother. Are you okay?"

Brittany burst into tears and started hugging me. I wrapped my arms around her and hugged her back.

"Don't cry. It's all over now."

While I was trying to help Brittany keep her composure, Nick called my phone and said that he was outside.

Before I hung up Nick said, "Aye, there's one more thing, Mike."

"What is it?"

Nick told me that by the time he had made it to Chinx's house, he was already dead. He said it looked like he had been decapitated while he sitting at the kitchen table.

Principles

"Damn," was all that I could say. I told Ale and Roc to take Brittany outside and that Nick should be out there waiting to take her to her mother. I don't know what it was or what had come over me. But, before I walked out of the room, I found myself just staring at the paint on the wall and wondering if I would ever be able to live a normal life. I wondered if I'd ever meet the right woman, settle down, and have kids. I wondered if when I was finished with the game, would the game be finished with me, too. Or, would this shit follow me forever?

***

As I stood in my living room staring through the window and drinking a shot of scotch, my phone rang. It was Katrina saying that she was at the front gate and needed me to let her in. I buzzed the gate open and I could see her turning into my driveway a moment later. She parked her car and walked toward the front door. Before Katrina could even knock or ring the doorbell, I sat my glass on the table, opened the door, and invited her inside. She began to tell me something, but I put my finger on her lips and stopped her.

"Let's have this discussion later," I said.

I gazed long and hard into her eyes and then I grabbed her waist, gently pulling her body against mine.

Principles

"I'm glad you're here," I said.

Then, I slowly kissed her soft lips as she wrapped her arms around my neck and began to kiss me back. I took her by the hand and guided her into the bedroom. Then, I laid her on the bed and commenced to kissing her again. I had taken off all my clothes and had begun undressing Katrina starting with her heels.

Once we were both naked, I made passionate love to her. While making long, slow strokes to the inside of her body, I noticed that tears had begun rolling down her face. With every stroke that I made, Katrina dug her nails deeper and deeper into my back, screaming louder and louder until the point of climax.

"Oh my God, Mike!" she exclaimed as she gasped for air.

She then rolled over and laid her head on my chest. She smiled at me and asked, "Why didn't we do this sooner?"

I told her that all of this was my fault. The first time we tried dating, I knew I wasn't emotionally ready for a commitment to anyone and I didn't want to play with her heart. I told her that God makes things happen according to His time and that we can't rush His timing.

"I completely agree. Thank you, Mike."

"Thanks for what, babe?" I asked.

"Thank you for being honest with yourself and me."

Principles

She waited for a second or two and then asked, "So, do you think you're ready now?"

While we were still lying in the bed wrapped underneath the covers, I gently grabbed Katrina by the hand.

"I couldn't be more ready," I said as I kissed her hand. "My home is now your home... Mi casa, su casa hermosa."

As I got up to go to the bathroom, my cell phone rang.

"See who's calling," I said.

It's Ale," she said.

"I need to leave. I'll be back later."

"Is it about Richblood?"

I said, "More than likely, babe."

"Just be careful, Mike."

I told her that I would as I got dressed and left to meet up with Ale and Roc.

Lesson 9:
What Goes Around Comes Around

As soon as I got inside my car, I called Ale and Roc on three-way. I told them that this shit with Richblood ends tonight.

"I have a plan. Ale, meet me at Roc's house."

Once we were all together at Roc's house, I asked Roc if he had gotten the van like I asked. He told me that he did.

Ale asked, "So, what's the plan to kill this muthafucka?"

"Simple… First, we're going to locate every major spot RichBlood does business. I want to target his trap houses, his corners, his hitters, and his soldiers. I wanna cripple this muthafuckas organization."

Roc said, "What about RichBlood? Once we start killing off his people, he's got to know that he's next."

Ale said, "Yeah, Mike, killing Richblood won't be easy if he knows we're coming for him."

"Don't worry, I have a plan for that, too."

I instructed Ale to get the van ready and I had Roc help me load up the straps and bulletproof vests. When we made it to the first location, there was a group of maybe fifteen to twenty of Richblood's soldiers standing in front of a corner liquor store. I told Ale to park in a nearby alley so we could sneak up on them.

"Mask up, and let's handle this shit."

We got out of the van and walked through the alley toward the group. I told them to make sure no one got away. Once we were close enough to RichBlood's Posse Boyz gang, we opened fire into the crowd trying to kill everyone in sight. I purposely intended for the store parking lot to look like a war zone. Once I felt like my mission was accomplished, we headed to the next location. The second location was the home of RichBlood's best hitter. I told Ale to park several houses down, stay in the van, and leave it running. I put my mask on and instructed Roc to come with me.

When we approached the house, we could see through the windows that the guy was sitting on his couch watching television. I told Roc that we were going to sneak inside through the back door. He picked the deadbolt on the backdoor, and we eased our way inside. I slowly crept to the back of the couch where the guy was seated. I cocked my revolver pistol and fired two shots to the back of the man's head. There was no warning, and I had felt zero remorse. The guy never knew what hit him.

I told Roc, "Close the curtains, and let's go."

Principles

Ale picked us up at the end of the driveway and sped off. The third location was one of Richblood's trap houses. I told Ale to drive by so I could scope everything out. I noticed a car parked in the driveway that had two guys sitting inside. I instructed Ale to circle back around and park a few houses down against the curb.

"Ale, two guys are sitting inside the car in the driveway. I want you to t-shirt their asses. Roc, you and I are going inside the house. I wanna lay everything in that muthafucka down like carpet."

After exiting the van we walked to Richblood's trap house. As soon as we made it to the driveway, Ale ran and jumped on top of the hood of the parked car that the guys were sitting in and began spraying bullets through the windshield like a mad man instantly killing both men inside of the car. Roc and I kicked in the front door of the house and started shooting everything in sight. Everyone scattered like cockroaches, trying to find cover. The more rounds we fired, the quicker the bodies dropped. I didn't come to bullshit. I came to send a message. The rifle that I was shooting held one hundred rounds, and I planned on using every single round.

When the gun smoke finally cleared, we walked back to the van and drove off. The fourth target was RichBlood's cousin and second-best hitter. We went to his home and

parked along the curb a few houses down.
Right before Ale got ready to turn the van off,
the guy walked out his front door heading to
his car. I told Ale to wait and let's just follow
him. We followed RichBlood's cousin maybe
three or four blocks until we got to a traffic
light. I was waiting for that right moment, and
I think we had just gotten it. I looked to make
sure no one was around, and then I told Ale to
pull right next to the hitter's car.

Once Ale made a complete stop, Roc
opened the sliding door on the van, and we
fired a horde of bullets into the man's car. We
slammed the sliding door back shut and sped
off, leaving Richblood's cousin slumped over
his steering wheel and his car riddled with
bullet holes. I told Ale and Roc that we needed
to ditch the van and find Richblood. We
parked the van in an alley, soaked the inside
with gasoline, and set it on fire to destroy any
trace of evidence. Then, we got inside Roc's car
and left the scene.

By now, RichBlood knew that he was
next, and we would eventually come for him. I
was certain that we wouldn't find him at his
mansion, so I had Nick and a few of my paid
associates on the police force help me find out
where RichBlood was hiding. I eventually got a
phone call saying that his car was spotted
uptown in a hotel parking garage. I told Roc
and Ale to get ready. When we drove into the
hotel parking garage, I told Roc and Ale that

Principles

Richblood was more than likely in an upstairs penthouse, so we needed to keep everything as quiet as possible.

"Roc, get in position and wait until I call you with the room location. Ale, get the silencers and come with me."

We walked into the hotel lobby. I told Ale to wait by the elevators as I headed toward the front desk.

The lady working the front desk asked, "May I help you?"

"Yes ma'am. I accidentally locked myself out of my room."

"What's your name?"

"Mr. Jean-Jacques."

"May I see your I.D.?"

I said, "I apologize but I left my I.D., wallet, and key card inside the penthouse when I accidentally locked myself out."

The lady said, "That's quite alright, Mr. Jacques. Here's your new key card."

I sarcastically said, "Thank you, ma'am. Your customer service is killer."

When Ale and I got on the elevator, I called Roc and told him that we were headed upstairs to the penthouse and that I needed him to get in position. Once we found Richblood's room, I put my ear to the door and tried listening for any signs that he was inside. I could hear him on the phone talking to someone. I asked Ale to wait outside by the door. Then, I slid the key card in and opened the door very carefully. As I closed the door, I could still hear Richblood in a back room talking on the phone.

By the time he walked out of the room, I was sitting at the kitchen bar having a drink. When he saw me, he stared at me for a brief second in disbelief.

I said, "I didn't know how long it was going to take you to come from the back, so I fixed myself a drink. I hope you don't mind."

RichBlood casually walked next to me, put his phone down on the kitchen counter, and said, "Mr. Michael Davis, you have some nerve coming here."

"Yeah, well you started this shit, and I'm just here to end it. I do agree that we gotta stop meeting under these circumstances."

He replied, "So help me understand… Do you really think that you can murder my people, bring down my organization, and get away with it, Mr. Davis?"

"All of this shit that went down tonight was your doing, RichBlood."

"I should have killed you when I had the opportunity."

"That's funny because that's the same thing Don Neto said right before I killed his ass. You see, the fact of the matter is that you did have an opportunity to kill me and didn't take it just like I have the opportunity to kill you right now at this very moment. Look down at your shirt. If I give the signal, that red dot on your chest will end all this shit tonight. I'm willing to let bygones be bygones, but you need to leave Texas tonight and never come back."

"Do you think I'm your dog? Do you think that you can tell me what to do and I just obey?"

I said, "Don't make me kill you. Your reign here was over long before it even began."

"If you kill me, you must be ready to dig many more graves," he said. "My people will hunt you down and collect the souls of everyone you have ever loved. Can you deal with that much blood on your hands, Mr. Davis?"

"You should know by now not to underestimate me. I'm capable of doing a lot more than you think." I looked Richblood in the eyes and said, "I'm giving you three hours to fucking leave. Period."

Then, I turned to walk away. As I stepped toward the door, I heard a click-clack sound. I said, "If I were you, I would put the gun down."

"If you were me, huh? That's just it, rude boy. You're not me, and you could never be me."

"I'm telling you, RichBlood, you don't want to do this."

"Stop ya begging bumbaclot and turn around to face me one last time. I relish looking a man in the eyes before I kill him."

Principles

As I slowly turned my body toward him, I suddenly heard a loud explosion and then the sound of shattering glass. Seconds later, I could see the window of the penthouse shatter into pieces, and RichBlood fell to the floor. Roc had shot through the window hitting him in the back of his head, killing him with one fatal shot and leaving his body lying in a pool of blood.

Ale ran through the door with his gun drawn and asked, "Are you okay, Mike? I heard a gunshot."

I said, "Yeah, I'm good, Ale."

As I turned to exit the room, I noticed that Richblood's phone was still on the kitchen counter. I picked it up and put it to my ear. I could hear someone slowly breathing on the other end of the phone. I took the phone away from my ear, looked at it, and then pressed the end call button.

Lesson 10:
Karma Has No Expiration Date

Here we are a month later. Katrina and I were finally in a much better place with each other. We were on a good path, and I was beginning to spend more quality time with her. I rented a beach house for the weekend and decided to surprise her with a romantic picnic on the beach. I hired a service to set everything up for us. We sat on a blanket in the sand drinking wine and watching the waves of the beautiful blue ocean water. We decided to take a stroll along the beach before walking back to the beach house.

Once we made it back to the beach house, she asked me if I could run to the store to get another bottle of wine and pick up a few small items while she finished relaxing.

"Of course, beautiful. You know I don't mind. I'll be right back."

As I walked toward my car, I noticed that there was something placed on the windshield. Once I got a closer look, I realized that it was a rose - a black rose. There was a note attached to it that read: "Mr. Davis, you came for the devil, and now the devil is coming for you." The message had me just standing there with a bewildered look on my face. Two seconds later, I heard a gunshot from inside the beach house. I ran inside as quickly as I could. When I opened the door, I saw Katrina standing over a body holding my gun. She was visibly afraid and shaken up. I walked to her and slowly eased my gun away from her hands. I put my arms around her and held her ever so tightly.

I spoke softly into her ear, "I'm sorry, baby. I'm sorry."

"He tried to attack me, Mike. I didn't know what else to do."

"Believe me, baby, you did the right thing. You did the right thing."

I continued holding her and reassured her that everything would be okay. Then, I took her by the hand and slowly walked her to the couch and sat her down. I walked back over to the man's dead body and bent down to remove the mask from his face. I also checked his pockets for any clues. When I reached into his shirt pocket, I pulled out a passport that indicated he had flown from the Caribbean islands. I rolled the guy's head to the side and saw a familiar sight. The man's neck was tatted with the Posse Boyz logo. I stood to my feet, grabbed my cell phone, and called Roc.

I said, "Roc, we have a fucking problem."

www.ingramcontent.com/pod-product-compliance
Lightning Source LLC
Chambersburg PA
CBHW070608180626
46817CB00005B/2049